Busy Bees

A Sensory Defensiveness Story

Abejas Ocupadas
Una Historia Sensorial de la Defensividad

Written by Marvie Ellis
Escrito por Marvie Ellis

Illustrated by Jenny Loehr
Ilustrado por Jenny Loehr

Published in 2008 — by Speech Kids Texas Press, Inc.
3802 Beaconsdale Drive
Austin, Texas 78727
ISBN: (978-1-933319-06-3) hardback
Library of Congress Card Number: 2006905041

Busy Bees / Written by Marvie Ellis; Illustrated by Jenny Loehr.
1 st. ed. - Austin, Texas.:Speech Kids Texas Press, Inc., © 2008.
32 p.: col. Ill.; 29 cm.
A Story about Sensory Defensiveness/ Hypersensitivity
Summary: A young girl tells how different things in our everyday environment can sometimes make our five senses upset. She explains how working with an occupational therapist helped her with overcoming a sensory dysfunction or hypersensitivity to food textures.
1. Sensory Integration Dysfunction - Juvenile fiction. 2. Sensory Defensiveness / Hypersensitivity - Juvenile fiction. 3. Disorders/ Disabilities - Juvenile fiction. 4. Multicultural - Juvenile fiction.
5. Spanish Translation - Juvenile fiction.
1. Ellis, Marvie, author. 2. Loehr, Jenny, ill. 3. Busy Bees. Title.

For inquiries about the author and information about
Speech Kids Texas Press, Inc., please visit our website at

www.speechkidstexaspress.com

Rita Mills—Book Packaging Consultant—The Book Connection
www.BookConnectionOnline.com
Victor Higginbotham—Cover Design

The paper used in this publication meets the requirements of the American National Standard for Permanence of Paper for Printed Library Materials Z39.48-1984.
Printed in China

Acknowledgements

Thank you my husband, Tellis and son, Brian for your love, support and patience. I love you very much.

Thank you my mentor / sister / friend, Karla Frazier, D.M.D., in Austin, for your tremendous encouragement and my bright teeth.

Thank you my sister, Lynn Harris and family for letting me read to you over the phone past bedtime.

Thank you my brother, Calvin Frazier, for being a great soundboard.

Thank you Mom (Mrs. Marvie Frazier) for without whom none of my business dreams could have been.

Thank you, Grandmas Tommie & MaMas, Grandpa Georgie, and my father-in-law, T.B. Ellis, III, M.D., for your daily prayers and encouragement.

Thank you, Dolly for your editing skills.

Thank you, Mrs. Maria L. Cruz for translating the stories.

Thank you very much, Mrs. Tayde Gladyn for your extra help with Spanish translation and editing skills.

Thank you, Jenny for having a special gift and sharing it with me.

Thank you, Rita Mills for your time, advice and contributions.

Thanks to all the parents and professionals who took the time and care to review the stories.

Most of all, thank you to all the children with ASD, you are most inspiring.

In remembrance of my father, Henry C. Frazier, Ph.D.
I love and miss you deeply.
May God bless and keep us.

Other Special Needs books by Marvie Ellis
Otros Libros Especiales de Necesidades por Marvie Ellis

Published in 2005

Keisha's Doors: An Autism Story
Las Puertas de Keisha: Una Historia de Autismo

2006 Benjamin Franklin Award Finalist
Finalista en el Premio de Benjamin Franklin 2006

Tacos Anyone? An Autism Story
¿Alguien Quiere Tacos? Una Historia de Autismo

2005 Barbara Jordan Media Award
Premio Barbara Jordan 2005

Forthcoming / Próximo

Sitting on Letters: A Story about Low Muscle Tone
Sentarse Sobre Letras: Una Historia sobre Tono Bajo del Músculo

Trouble Waiting: An Autism Story
Problemas a la Vista: Una Historia de Autismo

The Best Hello: An Autism Story
El Mejor Saludo: Un Libro de Historia sobre Autismo

My Lunch Buddy: A Friend with Cerebral Palsy
Mi Compañero de Almuerzo: Un Amigo con Parálisis Cerebral

My Voice, My Baby: A Story about Loudness
Mi Voz, Mi Bebé: Una Historia sobre Ruido Fuerte

Ready, Set, ….Go!: A Friend with Down Syndrome
¡En Sus Marcas, Listos,…Fuera!: Un Amigo con Síndrome de Down

Busy Bees

A Sensory Defensiveness Story

Abejas Ocupadas
Una Historia Sensorial de la Defensividad

One day, Mom and Dad were talking outside near our flower garden.

Un día Mamá y Papá estaban platicando afuera, cercas de nuestro jardín de flores.

A bee flew around Mom's head.

Una abeja voló alrededor de la cabeza de Mamá.

It didn't fly near Dad, so he kept talking.

Mom's eyes grew wide.

No voló cerca de papá, así es que el siguió platicando.

Los ojos de Mamá se pusieron muy grandes.

Se puso tan molesta por la abeja ocupada que zumbaba alrededor de su cabeza que dejó de escuchar lo que Papá le estaba diciendo. Cuando se fué la abeja, mi Papá le preguntó, "¿Porque no me escuchabas?"

She became so upset by the busy bee buzzing around her head that she stopped listening to what Dad was saying to her. When the bee flew away, Dad asked, "Why weren't you listening to me?"

Mom said, "I couldn't hear you. There was a bee buzzing near me."

Mi Mamá le dijo, "No podía escucharte. Habia una abeja que zumbaba cerca de mí."

Sometimes, different things in our environment can really upset our bodies.

A veces algunas cosas en nuestro medio ambiente pueden molestar mucho a nuestro cuerpo.

My occupational therapist, Ms. Lynn, calls it a "busy bee" moment. An occupational therapist works with kids who have "busy bee" moments with one or more of their five senses.

La Sra. Lynn, mi terapeuta ocupacional, le llama un momento de "abeja ocupada". Una terapeuta ocupacional da terapia a los niños que tienen momentos de "abejas ocupadas" con uno o más de sus cinco sentidos.

Each of our five senses—sight, touch, taste, smell, and hearing, can become so bothered that it can make us stop listening to others or even trying new experiences.

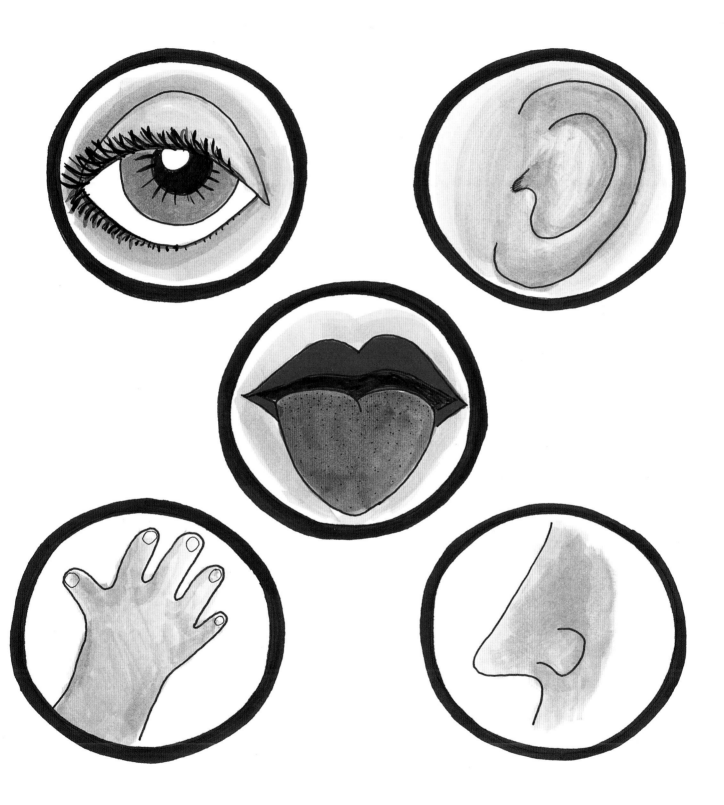

Cada uno de nuestros cinco sentidos—vista, tacto, gusto, olor, y oído, pueden molestarnos tanto que nos hace no poder escuchar a los demás o de tratar de tener nuevas experiencias.

For example, if bright lights bother your eyes, then the lights will be your "busy bees". The lights can make your head hurt or may make you blink a lot.

Por ejemplo, si la luz brillante molesta tus ojos, entonces las luces son las "abejas ocupadas". La luz puede que haga que tu cabeza te duela, o puede hacer que parpadees mucho.

If you don't like
getting your hands or
mouth dirty, your
"busy bee" could be
different textures you
touch or textures that
touch your skin.

Si no te gusta que se
te ensucien tus manos
o tu boca, tus "abeja
ocupada" pueden ser
texturas diferentes
que tocas, o texturas
que tocan tu piel.

This can happen with
certain food textures, like
soft, crunchy, or bumpy.

Wearing shirts with tags,
long sleeves, or pants
may bother your skin.

Esto también puede
suceder con ciertas
texturas de comida, como
suavidad, que sea
crujiente, o desigual.

Si usas camisas con
etiquetas, con mangas
largas, o hasta pantalones
pueden molestar tu piel.

My big sister has those "bees" around her every time she goes near a candle store. The candle scents make her head hurt.

Mi hermana mayor tiene esas "abejas" alrededor de ella cada vez que está cerca de alguna tienda de velas. Los olores de las velas hacen que le duela su cabeza.

Sometimes, "busy bees" can come from certain smells in the air like flowers or lotions.

A veces, "abejas ocupadas" pueden venir de ciertos olores en el aire, como flores o lociones.

Finally, loud noises or electronic toys may cause lots of "busy bees".

Finalmente, mucho ruido o jugetes electrónicos pueden provocar muchas "abejas ocupadas".

When I was little, I learned my busy bees buzzed most when I touched and smelled different foods. I was a very picky eater.

Cuando yo era pequeña, aprendí que mis abejas ocupadas zumbaban cuando yó tocaba y olía ciertas comidas. Yo era una comedora muy selectiva.

FIVE SENSES

1.
2.
3.
4.
5.

La Sra. Lynn me ayudó a aprender a conocer las texturas y las comidas que me molestaban.

La Sra. Lynn dice que es muy bueno conocer lo que hace que las "abejas ocupadas" zumben. Una terapeuta ocupacional, como ella, puede ayudar a que se vallan.

Ms. Lynn helped me learn which textures and foods bothered me.

Ms. Lynn says it's good to know what makes your "busy bees" buzz. An occupational therapist like her can help make them go away.

Crackers
Chicken Nuggets
Dry Cereal
Pasta
Broccoli
Peas
Drumstick
Mac & Cheese
Mixed fruit
Burger

She brushed my hands, arms, and legs. Then, we played in bowls filled with all types of food textures.

Ella cepilló mis manos, brazos, y piernas. Entonces, jugamos con platos ondos llenos de toda clase de comidas de diferentes texturas.

1.

2.

Al principio yo lloraba mucho. Pero después de algunas semanas de practica, me fué posible tocar y probar las comidas. Tenían muy buen sabor!

Mi diversión favorita ahora es jugar con masa de galletas y hacer toda clase de galletas. Quizás seré un panadero famoso de galletas.

At first, I cried a lot. But after a few weeks of practice, I was able to touch and taste the foods. They tasted pretty good!

My favorite hobby now is playing in cookie dough and making all types of cookies. I may become a famous cookie baker!

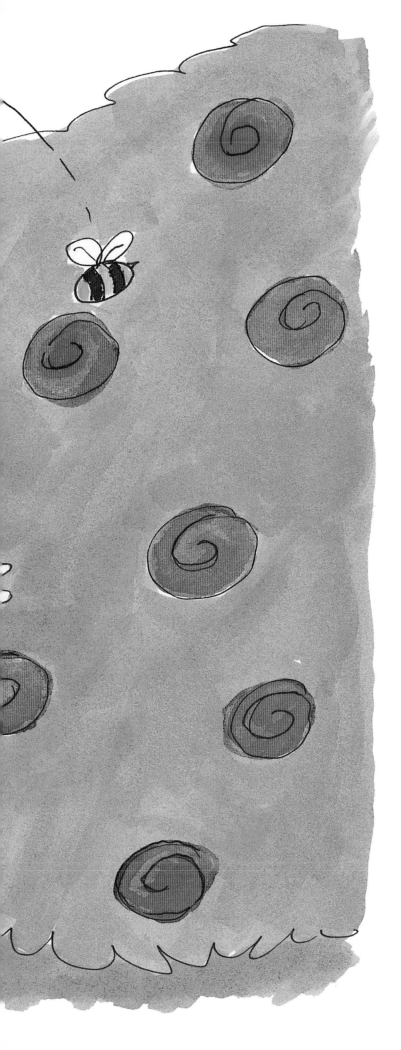

Whenever you feel
your bees starting to
buzz around you,
tell a grown up.
They can help you
and keep the "bees"
from buzzzz-ing.

Cuando sientas que
las abejas
comienzen a zumbar
a tu alrededor, dile a
alguna persona
adulta. Ellos te
pueden ayudar a
mantener las
"abejas" lejos de
zummmmbar.

Professional Reviews / Revisiones Profesionales

"Nice analogy for kids to understand what it means to be over stimulated from various types of sensory input."
—Lori Hickman, M.S., OTR/L, SIPT Certified
(STARS—Student Therapies and Resource Services) Phoenix, Arizona

"Buena analogía para que los niños entiendan lo que significa estar sobre estimulado en varios tipos de entradas sensoriales."
—Lori Hickman, M.S., OTR/L. Certificación SIPT No. 1528,
STARS (Student Therapies and Resource Services—Terapias de Estudiantes y Servicios Profesionales), Phoenix, AZ

"I loved the concept of 'busy bees' and its tie to OT. It has potential to help our high functioning students to better understand their 'meltdowns' that are related to sensory."
—Barbara A. Booth, Ph.D., BCBA, Behavior Specialist, Pflugerville, Texas

"Me gusta el concepto de 'abejas ocupadas' y su conección a la terapia de reeducación basada en trabajos manuales. Tiene potencial para ayudar a nuestros estudiantes que funcionan mejor a entender sus 'fusiones' que están relacionados con problemas sensoriales."
—Barbara A. Booth, Ph.D., BCBA, Pflugerville, Texas

"How delightful the phrase 'busy bee' is to describe things in our environment that bother us. We all have some type of 'busy bee' in our lives and this story illustrates this well."
—LaQuinta Khaldun, M.S., CCC-SLP,
owner of Carolina Speech Services, Charlotte, North Carolina

"La frase 'abejas ocupadas' es encantadora y describe cosas que nos molestan en nuestro medio ambiente. Todos tenemos algún tipo de 'abeja ocupada' en nuestras vidas y esta historia lo ilustra muy bien."
—LaQuinta Khaldun, M.S., CCC-SLP,
dueña de Carolina Speech Services, Charlotte, Carolina Del Norte

"…the story does a nice job of making an analogy that people can understand to help them understand the sensory issues for many children…."
—Hope Korbet, M.S., CCC-SLP,
Kennedy Krieger Institute, Center for Autism and Related Disorders,
Baltimore, Maryland

"…la historia describe muy bien la analogía que las personas pueden entender y a su vez ayudar a entender los problemas sensoriales de muchos niños incluyendo los niños autistas."

—Hope Korbet, M.S., CCC-SLP,
Instituto Kennedy Krieger, Centro para Autismo y Deshabilidades
Relacionadas con el Autismo, Baltimore, MD

"These stories are sensitive, informative, and creative. Marvie Ellis utilizes unique examples that specifically address sensory and motor weaknesses often seen in children …. I would recommend these stories for parents, children, educators, and occupational therapists."

—Christine T. Barry, Ph.D., Pediatric Neurophysiologist,
Associate Professor of Pediatrics, Division of Behavioral Pediatrics and
Psychology, Case Western University, School of Medicine, Cleveland, Ohio

"Estas historias son sensibles, dan información y son creativas. Marvie Ellis utiliza ejemplos unicos que hablan específicamente de las debilidades sensoriales y de motor que a menudo tienen algunos niños. Recomiendo estas historias a los padres, niños, educadores y terapistas ocupacionales."

—Christine T. Barry, Ph.D., Neuropsicologa de Pediatría,
Profesora Asociada en Pediatría, Departamento de Comportamiento
y Psicología Pediátrica, Case Western University, Escuela de Medicina,
Cleveland, OH

"This story explains in easy terms the distracting effects of certain sensory experiences for some people. The analogy of the bee as a sensory distraction is very clever. Sensory issues are difficult to understand even for professionals, and this story goes a long way in clarifying what exactly these issues are like for people who have them."

—Kapila Seshadri, M.D., Associate Professor of Pediatrics, Section Head,
Section of Neurodevelopment Disabilities, Department of Pediatrics,
UMDNJ- Robert Wood Johnson Medical School, New Jersey

"Esta historia explica en términos fáciles los efectos de distracción de ciertas experiencias sensoriales para algunas personas. La analogía de la abeja como distracción sensorial es muy astuta. Las ediciones sensoriales son difíciles de entender incluso para los profesionales, y esta historia nos ayuda perfectamente a clarificar como es que son estos problemas para las personas que los padecen."

—Kapila Seshadri, M.D., Profesor Asociado de Pediatría, Director de Sección,
Sección de Deshabilidades de NeuroDesarrollo, Departamento de Pediatría,
UMDNJ—Robert Wood Johnson Medical School, New Jersey

About the Author:

Marvie Ellis received her Bachelor of Science degree in Communicative Disorders from Jackson State University in Jackson, Mississippi and her Master of Science degree from the University of North Carolina at Chapel Hill (1996). She has specialized training in working with the birth to five population, children with autism spectrum disorders, speech-language delays, oral motor therapy, play based therapy, sensory therapy, and behavior modification techniques. Marvie provides trainings and seminars to parents and educators nationally. She is a member of the American Speech-Language and Hearing Association, the Texas Speech-Language and Hearing Association, and the Autism Society of America. Marvie lives in Austin with her husband, Tellis and son, Brian. She enjoys writing stories, supporting others in their entrepreneurial and quiet moments for meditation.

Sobre La Autora:

Marvie Ellis obtuvo su Licenciatura en Ciencias en Desórdenes de Comunicación de la Universidad de Jackson en Jackson, Mississippi y su Maestría de Licenciatura en Ciencias de la Universidad de Carolina del Norte en Chapel Hill (1996). Se ha especializado trabajando con niños que tienen desórdenes de autismo, habla y lenguaje retrasado, terapia de motor oral, terapia basada en juegos, terapia sensorial, y técnicas modificando comportamientos de niños desde su nacimiento hasta los cinco años. Marvie es una altavoz nacional y asesora de padres y educadores. Es miembro de la Asociación Americana del Habla y Lenguaje, Asociación de Texas del Habla-Lenguaje y Oído y la Sociedad de Autismo de America. Marvie vive en Austin con su esposo, Tellis e hijo, Brian. Le gusta escribir historias, para ayudar a personas en sus ocupaciones y momentos de meditación.

About the Illustrator:

Jenny Loehr obtained her Master of Arts degree in Speech Pathology in northern California at Humboldt State University in 1990. She has been practicing art and illustration three times as long as she has been a clinician, and recently been able to "marry" the two professions by opening Curly Girl Studios where she illustrates books and materials for the speech-language pathology and audiology community. Jenny spends her days illustrating and practicing speech pathology in Austin, Texas where she lives with her husband Brian, and her two boys, Jacob and Joshua.

Sobre La Ilustradora:

Jenny Loehr obtuvo su Maestría de Arte en Patología del Habla en la Universidad Humboldt en el Norte de California en 1990. Ha ejercido su arte e ilustración tres veces más tiempo que el tiempo que ha ejercido en clínicas, y recientemente ha podido combinar sus dos profesiones en sus Curly Girl Studios, ilustrando libros y documentos para la comunidad especializada en patología del habla-lenguaje y audiología. Jenny pasa sus días ilustrando y practicando patología del habla en Austin, Texas, donde vive con su esposo Brian, y sus dos hijos, Jacob y Joshua.